AF253370

FOOTPRINTS

An Anthology of
Poems and Short Stories

KEMERA MOODLY

First Edition, 2020
ISBN: 978-0-620-85162-6
E-ISBN: 978-0-620-85163-3

Published by Kemera Moodly

DEDICATION

For Mum and Dad.

____

ACKNOWLEDGEMENTS

My parents - thank you for your unconditional
love and support, for always believing in me
and encouraging me to continue writing.

Greg Ardé - thank you for your invaluable editing
and sound advice (to include your crucial
contribution to the murder scene) - I sincerely
appreciate all of your insight and guidance.

Alan Cooper - thank you for your edit and review of the
anthology - your corrections and tips were helpful.

Megan Guyt - thank you for your time, effort and the
many back-and-forth edits to the design and all my
content changes - I appreciate all your endeavours
to make my anthology look and feel just right.

A NOTE TO THE READER

Throughout life's journey people walk into and out of our lives leaving footprints on our hearts. They make a lasting impression, tenderly touch our souls, give life greater meaning, renewing our spirits. They open our eyes to something beautiful we've been blind to before. Some of these people are dear to us and are here to stay, while others may come for a short period to teach us a hard lesson. We need to let them go once the lesson has imparted.

Whatever the reason, always embrace those people who leave impressions on your heart for they gently carve you into the person you are. They unintentionally give you a fraction of their wisdom, love, joy, anger, heartache and pain.

As the poems, essays and stories in this anthology are a testament to, my heart has been shaped and influenced by my interaction with people whose paths I've crossed. Sometimes the footprints have been gentle, sometimes deeper. Perhaps it was a passing glance, a fleeting smile, a distant observation or intense connection.

Whatever it may be, my spirit was renewed, and my eyes were opened to some previously unknown beauty and I've attempted to express my emotions and these experiences as accurately and as fully as possible. I can only hope that my fourth anthology will inspire you and leave gentle footprints on your heart.

CONTENTS

DEDICATION   I

ACKNOWLEDGEMENTS   III

A NOTE TO THE READER   V

SHORT STORIES

15:30 AT THE LIGHTHOUSE   3

TEARS IN MUNNAR (PART 1)   19

TEARS IN MUNNAR (PART 2)   25

FORBIDDEN LOVE IN KOVALAM   39

POETRY

MY ETERNAL SUN, MY ETERNAL MOON   55

YOUR FOOTPRINTS ON MY HEART (PART 1)   57

A SONNET FOR LAKE VEMBANAD   58

LITTLE BIRD   59

DON'T BE AFRAID   60

IF YOU GIVE ME THE TWILIGHT SKY 61

IF THE BIRDS STOP SINGING 62

THE OLD TURKISH LADY 64

YOUR FOOTPRINTS ON MY HEART (PART 2) 65

THE MAESTRO 66

THE BACKWATERS OF POOVAR 67

FADO 68

AN ODE TO GRANADA 69

ESSAYS

MEMORIES OF GRANDFATHER GEORGE
AND THE FOOTPRINTS HE LEFT ON MY SOUL 73

ESTHER'S PRAYER 79

SATURDAYS AT MY GRANDMOTHER'S TABLE 85

SHORT STORIES

"Experience the flow of life not
through the narrow lens of the mind,
but through the vast refuge of the heart"

— BRYANT MCGILL

15:30 at the lighthouse

"When you are sorrowful look again in your heart, and you shall see that in truth you are weeping for that which has been your delight"

KHALIL GIBRAN

Kovalam, Kerala, South India - September 2016.

Neela stands at the water's edge, staring at the vast azure ocean before her. The tide is rising. The sky darkens to a deep indigo hue. She has waited patiently for two hours for someone to join her on the shores of Kovalam beach. It's almost 17:45 and the light begins to shine from the tall, red and white striped lighthouse a few metres behind her. She knows he will not come. With teary eyes and a burdened heart, she turns and walks away.

One can only understand the heartache Neela feels here at the Kovalam lighthouse if her story is told.

***

Kovalam - February 2015.

Neela Chettiar, a 24-year-old English teacher from Kovalam, a pretty seaside town in the state of Kerala, never knew what it meant to be in love. The romance of Bollywood was a fantasy too distant, too unreal to ever resemble something that could happen in her lifetime. She resented the picture perfect love stories that the film industry sold to communities around India and the world, and which most young girls her age voraciously consumed. She knew, from personal experience, that romance of that nature simply did not exist. She knew that those male characters who were unconditionally loving and caring were by no means an accurate portrayal of men in real life. In reality, these characters were the opposite of what men were to women.

Neela was raised by her mother since the age of 10. After 12 years of violent abuse at the hands of her husband, Neela's mother could not withstand the relentless assaults any longer and divorced him. They moved out of their home with nothing but a single suitcase of clothes. Neela knew from a tender age that love was evidently not the grandiose picture Bollywood painted - love was not about those melodic, stirring songs of a couple's undying love for each other, which they sing whilst chasing one another in picturesque pastures.

She knew that finding true love was simply a matter of chance, fate, serendipity, karma perhaps. But it would certainly not be something bestowed upon everyone, least of all Neela. She grew to be distrustful of male folk, unwilling to view them in a positive light, unwilling to view them as capable of feeling or showing love and more importantly, respect to women. What Neela did not know was that these tainted perceptions would change so drastically within a few months.

***

Neela earned her living at a renowned primary school in the nearby city of Trivandrum (officially named Thiruvananthapuram). Her students adored her and keenly looked forward to her lessons. She patiently taught them the English language and relished the moment, after months of hard work, when they were able to master their primary-level fluency in the language.

Every day after school, Neela returned to her mother, Vibha, in their home in Kovalam, 18 kilometres from Trivandrum. Her mother was exceptionally proud of her daughter and all her achievements, especially of her social standing in the community as a teacher. Teachers in India are revered for they are the providers, the conveyors of knowledge. There is a saying used by locals: "He who teaches one to read and write is God himself."

Neela and her mother were not only mother and daughter, they were the best of friends - they were each other's pillars of strength. They valued each other tremendously and the bond between them was so very close. But there was one sore point in their relationship - Vibha wanted nothing more for her daughter than to find her a decent and loving husband. Neela on the other hand wanted nothing more than to focus on her career as a teacher and achieve her mission to improve the lives of her students by delivering a high level of education. Marriage was certainly not on her radar. Finding a husband was not a priority for Neela even more so after she had witnessed the traumatic abuse her mother had endured at the hands of her father. She chose to dedicate her life to educating children, uplifting their lives and caring for her aging mother. Those were her only priorities in life.

But life can be serendipitous, especially when least expected. Neela's school was in the community spotlight in Trivandrum. Some of the students in her English class had entered a national poetry contest and two of her 10-year-old students had successfully earned a spot representing the school and the city as one of the Top Five Primary School Poets in the country. The local newspaper arranged to meet with Neela and the two students for a front page interview. And unbeknown to Neela, this newspaper article written in February 2015 would change her life as she knew it.

***

Neela arranged for the interview with the newspaper's journalist to take place at the school on a Monday afternoon after school closed. The students were fidgety, anxious to answer the questions as per their brief from the principal and their parents. As they waited in the school hall, Neela told them jokes to calm them down - she made them laugh out loud as the journalist entered.

Manivasan Balasubramanian introduced himself as the journalist from and warmly greeted Neela and the two students. To ease them into the interview, he questioned the children about irrelevant topics such as their favourite foods, their favourite cartoon characters and the books they've been allocated to read for the school term. Neela marvelled at how easily Manivasan engaged with them, how he made them laugh so effortlessly and made them feel at ease with him, despite being a perfect stranger.

In the space of a few minutes the interview was complete. Satisfied with their responses (which were somewhat spontaneous and off script), he allowed them to run off and join their parents who were eagerly waiting in the foyer. He suddenly turned his attention to Neela and as his eyes reached hers, she felt self-conscious and blushed uncontrollably. In a split second she realized how handsome he was, how his eyes glowed and how naturally his lips curled into a striking smile.

He smiled broadly at her as he said, "Well Ms. Neela Chettiar, you have certainly done a brilliant job with those two. Their attitude towards the English language and English literature and poetry is remarkably mature for children their age. I'm impressed!"

Neela blushed again and felt an intense heat rise into her flawless, olive-toned cheeks. Unsure what to say, she simply replied, "Thank you Mr. Balasubramanian. I am passionate about teaching these children English."

"Please, call me Mani. So can I perhaps chat with you and get to know exactly what it is you do to inspire such enthusiasm and passion in your students?"

Neela knew that the newspaper interview did not require her involvement, only her presence as support for the children. Confused, she asked Mani, "I beg your pardon sir, but I believe the interview is over and I was not required by my principal or your editor to respond to any questions."

Surprised by her hostility, Mani reassured her, "Ms. Chettiar, yes of course the interview is over. I was just curious about your role in inspiring the children. I just wanted to know a bit more about you as their teacher, off the record of course."

Neela stared at him blankly, uncertain of how she should respond. She was perceptive enough to know that he was displaying interest in her as a young woman and wanted to get to know more about her as a person. Never before had she been approached in this manner by a young man, simply because she had never before given anyone the opportunity to get this close to her, to get her to this stage of a conversation.

She hesitated, and sensing her tentativeness, he asked, "I am also a lover of the English language as well as poetry, so naturally I'm curious about the type of literature and poetry you enjoy reading. Perhaps, you may even write your own poetry?"

Neela pulled her eyes away from his face, completely unsure of how she should respond. Never before had she given a young man this much of an opportunity to engage with her, to question her, to display this much interest in her. Inexperienced and uncertain, she stammered "Yes. Yes. I. I do write a bit of po - poetry."

"Ahh, I knew you were a poet! You have this calm and collected demeanour that tells of a creative spirit. You seem like someone who will appreciate the work of Rumi and Shakespeare. May I ask you to accompany me for a cup of coffee, and we can chat about poetry a bit more?"

For the first time in her life Neela felt that her head and her heart were pulling her in two very different directions. Her head was saying she should not be so easily fooled by the pleasantries and bold friendliness of this stranger, while her heart was slowly being charmed by the seemingly genuine warmth and magnetic personality of this handsome and educated man standing before her.

Neela decided to follow her heart that day and indeed it certainly led her down a beautiful and unforgettable path.

***

After the very first coffee date, Mani and Neela found themselves walking towards the Vilinjam lighthouse, commonly referred to as the Kovalam lighthouse. As they sauntered towards this renowned landmark, a connection sparked and a friendship began. Mani and Neela began seeing each other more frequently. Soon enough, the budding friendship that had developed between the two lovers of poetry, blossomed into something more. Their relationship became a little more affectionate and tender - they grew closer and the connection they shared grew more intense over time.

They met each other, without fail, every day at 15:30 at the Kovalam lighthouse. School closed at 15:00 and Neela made her way on an auto rickshaw from Trivandrum to Kovalam. She walked the last few metres to the lighthouse and enjoyed the sea breeze blowing through her dark brown hair as she approached the little bench situated alongside the lighthouse. Mani would also make his way from Trivandrum, usually after he had submitted his article for the next morning's newspaper.

They would spend almost two hours every afternoon talking to one another about everything that they could possibly think about - the English language; the various elements of poetry; renowned poets they loved and were inspired by; Indian politics; the education system; human rights issues; and even new English words that they happened upon during the course of the day. On many an occasion they recited their favourite poems to one another with utter passion and delight.

It would start with Mani's simple question, "A penny for your thoughts my sweet Neela?" To which Neela would reply, "Right now I'm remembering the words of Rumi's poem , shall I recite it Mani?" And the conversation would flow.

Their time together at the lighthouse was a time in which they connected, engaged and became closer as friends and partners. They identified with one another in a way they could not with others. Their literary creativity and passion was shared as was their determination to teach, promote and shed light on the wonder of English literature.

Neela shared her deepest secrets, her dreams and desires, her anxieties and fears with Mani, as did he with her. He soon came to know that she distrusted male folk and that she had questioned men's supposed integrity and respect for women because of her experiences with her own father. He came to know her reasons why she had shunned men all through her life and understood her position as a young woman determined to be independent, empowered and strong.

But nothing could have prepared Neela for the part of Mani that she soon came to know. He shared with her the memories of his time as a journalist in war ravaged countries reporting on the armed conflict, death, devastation and humanitarian crises in Syria, Iraq and Palestine. Mani was scarred and deeply traumatized by all that he had witnessed as a foreign correspondent for eight years. He was broken on the inside, and when he returned to his home country he had made it his mission as a journalist to report on only the positive stories of his fellow citizens. He wanted to report the narratives of hope, joy and success which are often bypassed by most journalists in their effort to focus primarily on the negative.

Despite his efforts, Mani would often withdraw from those around him, even Neela. On those days when he was feeling down, Neela would try her best to lift his spirits. She would tell him silly jokes or buy him his favourite chocolate or even prepare his favourite sweetmeat, burfi. She would even sing a famous song from a Bollywood film, something that would always make him laugh because he knew how much she disliked those songs.

There were days when he would respond with laughter and the cloud of darkness would leave his face and his eyes would brighten again. But there were days when nothing she could say or do would cheer him up no matter how hard she tried. Mani would just stare blankly at the ocean, lost in his own serious thoughts. Those days were the days when Neela realized all she could do was sit alongside Mani and somehow comfort him with her silent presence.

***

No matter how many days and months passed, no matter how much joy or sadness they felt in their individual hearts, no matter how merciless the winter sun or how incessant the monsoon rain, Neela and Mani would not allow a single day to pass without meeting one another at precisely 15:30 at the Kovalam lighthouse. It was an inflexible habit, a daily ritual that could not be broken, for if it broke, it would mean that their relationship as they knew it, would cease.

Neela had taken Mani home to visit her mother a few times and Vibha was ecstatic with her daughter's choice of suitor. He met all of Vibha's criteria for her daughter, so she effortlessly pampered him with her motherly love and fed him copious amounts of biryani, masala chai and pistachio burfi whenever he visited. Vibha considered him to be the son that she never had, even before the relationship between Neela and Mani could be formalized. Vibha was simply overwhelmed with joy for her daughter, that Neela had finally found the happiness she so deserved.

But just as life can be serendipitous and fulfilling, it can also be so callous and unjust.

***

Kovalam - March 2016.

Neela and Mani continued to meet each other at the lighthouse every day at 15:30. But for many weeks, Neela had observed that Mani was growing quieter and more withdrawn. Their conversations were becoming shorter and less cheerful. They no longer spoke about poetry and literature as passionately as they once did. They no longer jovially exchanged jokes or laughed as unpretentiously as they once did. Neela felt the distance between herself and Mani growing greater every day. And all she could do was watch him slowly slip into a depression that was beyond her control. Nonetheless she tried to reassure him with her gentle presence and held his hand lovingly in hers as they wordlessly looked out into the ocean.

On one such day, Mani said to her in a rare moment of clarity and openness, "Neela, I sometimes wonder what it would be like to take all of the sorrow and pain that I have witnessed in the Middle East and release it deep into the ocean. The ocean is so vast - I'm sure it can handle the burden of all my sorrow and distress and all the sorrow I have witnessed in others. I want to know what it would feel like to be as light as the seagull soaring through the blue sky."

Neela did not know how to best respond to him. His sudden disclosure had caught her off guard. All she could do was hold his hand tighter and she told him, "Mani, you can choose to let go of the sorrow and pain if you choose to, you don't have to carry the burden of those emotions anymore, perhaps now is the time for you to let it go. Maybe you need to consider seeing a counsellor? They will know how to help you better than I or anyone in your family can."

Neela had taken advantage of the opportunity and finally had plucked up the courage to suggest to Mani that he needed to seek professional help. But he simply shrugged off the recommendation and blankly stared out into the ocean, lost in his own thoughts and emotions. He had done the same with his family. They had advised Neela how, ever since he had returned from his work as a foreign correspondent reporting on the war and conflict in the Middle East, he had slowly fallen into this harrowing depression that none of them could help him out of. He had repeatedly refused professional help from any doctor, psychiatrist or psychologist. They had said to her on many occasions that she was the only reason Mani would smile and show some sign of joy or contentment.

And so, when Mani refused to even consider what Neela had merely suggested, it came as no surprise to her. She knew he was opposed to receiving professional help, so she found herself grappling for some form of solution to the distress that Mani was experiencing.

Days and weeks passed and still there was no sign of improvement in Mani's psychological condition. Neela made it her duty to try every possible means to breathe new life into Mani. She recited poems both had never perused, from Omar Khayyam to Rabindranath Tagore, to Rudyard Kipling and Percy Shelley. She penned new poems solely for him and whispered them sweetly into his ear while they sat holding hands by the lighthouse. She made all his favourite treats to eat and religiously packed them into a picnic basket every day - pistachio burfi, sticky jalebi, masala chai, Malabar paratha, potato pakoras. She even attempted to teach him the complex art of origami. She taught him, like she would the children in her school, how to create leaping frogs and soaring cranes from a mere sheet of paper. The paper birds would float high up with the wind, towards the top of the lighthouse and once the ocean breeze died down, the birds would descend and flop onto Mani's shoes, making both laugh.

Soon she realized that everything she did was a fleeting distraction, a transitory diversion from the ever-present depression. Eventually, all she could do was speak to the only Force that could help Mani: God. She prayed for Mani to rise from the dark hole of this depression, to have light shine once more through him. She prayed for him to look at the world with new eyes, to see the beauty all around him, to marvel at the little glories in life - the tweet of a sparrow, the sound of the waves, the striking colour of a rose, the far-reaching, guiding light of a lighthouse, the innocent, carefree smile of a child. It was all Neela could do: pray.

***

Kovalam Beach - May 2016.

On a dull, rainy Wednesday during the mid-term school holidays, Neela knew that the showers would not keep Mani away from the lighthouse. It was monsoon season, but he had insisted that they visit the lighthouse every day just for 20 minutes. The rain was incessant, so at 15:15 she picked up her umbrella and slipped on her raincoat. The auto rickshaw dropped her off as close as possible to the lighthouse. From that point, she could see that Mani was not at their usual spot - the bench was unoccupied. The entire promenade was deserted. The rain had driven everyone indoors, and would have probably kept Mani indoors as well. Nonetheless, she looked at her watch - it was only 15:25, so she decided to wait for him just in case he arrived. She did not want to disappoint him if he arrived and she was not already there waiting for him.

And so, Neela stood in the shelter of the towering lighthouse, waiting for Mani. The rain pelted hard against her raincoat, against her unshielded face. But in her heart, she knew he would come. He always came - even on their crazy visits during the monsoon, he always kept to his word. The minutes ticked by and Neela felt the cold from the rain and the wind bite into her bones. The waves crashed dangerously behind her. It was 15:38 and still no sign of Mani. She looked at her phone - no missed calls, no text messages. She decided to call him on his mobile phone but there was no answer. She called his home, his mother answered and said that he had left to meet Neela at the lighthouse but that he should have arrived at the beach long ago, as he had left earlier than usual.

As his mother relayed this information to her, Neela grew worried but she reassured his mother (and herself) that the auto rickshaw could have broken down or had a minor accident in the rain, which would explain Mani not arriving on time. She ended the call and tucked the phone deep into her pocket. She scanned the area around the lighthouse. There was not one person in sight. The area where auto rickshaws parked was deserted. All the benches along the promenade were unoccupied.

For some reason, she decided to turn around and look at the ocean.

There was not a single fishing boat at sea - the boats were a familiar sight on the water. The water was turbulent and unforgiving in its rough back and forth movement. Suddenly Neela saw a neon green object bob in the undulating water about six metres away from the shore. She felt a rush of blood to her head. Her heart pounded heavily in her chest. She knew that Mani owned a neon green raincoat which he wore every day to the lighthouse during the monsoon season. She reassured herself that it could not be him, that he was not suicidal. But deep down, she knew that it was his body bobbing in the tempestuous ocean, that his depression and post-traumatic stress from his time in the Middle East had taken its eventual toll on him.

She called out to him, "Mani! Mani! Can you hear me? I will get help!"

Desperate, she called out for help in vain, knowing that there was nobody around to hear. There had been no lighthouse keeper in the lighthouse for a few years - the light was automated and worked on a daylight sensor system. There was not a soul to help Neela to rescue Mani.

Neela cried as the enormity of the situation gradually occurred to her. She frantically tried to call the Indian Coast Guard. Within half an hour help came, but it was too late. All they were able to do was recover his lifeless body from the turbulent sea. There was no pulse as they laid his body gently down onto the ground near the lighthouse, and they called the police to report the suicide and take a statement from Neela, the person who had first caught sight of the body in the water.

By 16:35, the sky had started to darken and the automated lighthouse sensed the diminishing daylight and the bright light began to shine out into the ocean. Neela was distraught. Kneeling at his side with tears streaming down her face, Neela's only thought was that the light from the Kovalam lighthouse was guiding Mani from this life into the next.

***

Kovalam - September 2016.

Four months have passed since that fateful day when Mani gave his life to the raging ocean. Not a day goes by without Neela visiting the Kovalam lighthouse at 15:30. She sits on the bench near the lighthouse and reflects on the many moments of laughter, love, joy, sorrow and silence that both she and Mani shared in the shadow of the towering lighthouse, gazing out into the vast azure Arabian Sea.

And for as long as she lives, she will visit the lighthouse daily to pay homage to Mani and the immense love and light that he had given her for so many months. She will visit the lighthouse to reminisce on all the beautiful moments that she shared with Mani. And, alas, she will always be haunted by the fact that she could not help him to overcome the depression that he experienced for so long, that she could have given him a little more love that would perhaps have allowed him to sit alongside her today.

Tears in Munnar (Part 1)

*"How lucky I am to have something
that makes saying goodbye so hard"*

WINNIE THE POOH

Indhu looks out into the sprawling green valley below. She is mesmerized by the valley's unsurpassed beauty. The faint white light of dawn sweeps across the sleeping valley and the silent mountains of Munnar, dispelling the dark obscurities of the fading night.

The peace at daybreak always stills her restless mind and prepares her for the day ahead. She tucks a few strands of her flowing black hair behind her ear, tightens her bun, neatens the pleats of her emerald saree and slowly makes her way down the path towards the tea plantation.

Indhu knows today will be unlike any other day. Her heart beats steadily but she knows that this calm will not last long. Prasoon will be waiting for her at the end of her shift. Indhu is ready to give him her heart and soul. He is all her heart yearns for and desires. But it will come at a price.

To have Prasoon means that she has to give up her family. No matter how ardently she has pleaded with them, they will not accept Prasoon into their home. He is Christian. Indhu knows that her parents would be happy only if she had chosen a Hindu boy. But the heart is blind to race, class, caste and faith. And Indhu's heart chose Prasoon, as his heart chose her.

Her father's words sting to this day even though he had said them almost a year ago. "If you choose him Indhu, you are no one to me, you are no one to this family. You will leave this house and you can never come back. You choose."

His callous words still echo in Indhu's head. She knows that no matter how painful it may be, she cannot live with those who are blinded by religious intolerance. She has only one choice - to be with Prasoon.

She nears the tea plantation and sees Jeena waiting for her at the gate. Jeena, her best friend since childhood, has been working alongside Indhu on the Kanan Devan Hills plantation since the age of 16. Forced to leave school by their conservative families, they have been contributing to the household income for the past eight years.

Picking tea has become a way of life for them both, and perhaps a little window of freedom away from their strict fathers. A time to socialize with other women their age, a time to take great delight in simply inhaling the clear, unblemished air of Munnar, a time to allow their childhood friendship to blossom, to share their secrets, their dreams, hopes and fears.

But today is the last day Indhu will ever have with sweet Jeena. She will say goodbye to her best friend, she will say goodbye to the tea plantation, to her beautiful Munnar. She will walk away only with the precious memories of life in this lush haven. She will walk away with the splendour of Munnar locked in her heart forever.

"Indhu! Why are you staring at the sky like that silly? The sun will hurt your eyes!"

Jeena walks over to Indhu and weaves her arm into Indhu's. Carefree, easy-going Jeena. Nothing ever seems to worry her. Indhu on the other hand carries the weight of the world on her shoulders. It tells on her face - the crinkling frown lines on her forehead, the solemn expression and the darkening circles under her eyes.

"Today is a beautiful day Indhu, so please smile. Don't look so serious *priyappetta* (dear)."

Her loving tone strikes a chord in Indhu. Tears fill her eyes and she pulls away from Jeena and walks hurriedly through the plantation gates and almost sprints to the change rooms.

She hears Jeena yell from behind, "Indhu, what's wrong?"

How will Indhu tell her? How will she tell Jeena that Prasoon and her are to elope this evening, to run away to Cochin, that they will get married in a Catholic church, that she will no longer be a Hindu? How will she tell Jeena that they may move to another state, most likely Tamil Nadu and they will never ever return to Munnar? How will she break Jeena's heart? How?

She wipes away the tears so Jeena does not see her sadness and swiftly changes into the blue saree uniform of the plantation. Jeena rushes into the change room and runs to Indhu.

"Indhu, why are you crying?"

Oh Jeena, nothing can ever be kept secret from her. Always so observant, so perceptive. Jeena lifts Indhu's chin with her index finger and looks her in the eye.

"Indhu what are you not telling me *priyappetta?*"

The tears fall across Indhu's face without reservation. She rests her head on Jeena's shoulder and weeps inconsolably onto the pallu of her saree. Through an endless stream of tears and sobs she manages to tell Jeena of the future she and Prasoon have decided upon.

With tears in her eyes, Jeena grips Indhu firmly and says "Indhu if this is what your heart desires, follow your heart *priyappetta*. I cannot be selfish and ask you to stay. Go Indhu, you have my blessing."

The two friends embrace one another in tears.

"But promise me that today I will see you smile your beautiful smile Indhu, okay? No more tears."

Indhu nods and together they set off into the tea fields to work side by side under the bright Keralan sun one last time.

***

As dusk approaches, Indhu wipes away the beads of sweat on her forehead. She picks up the last basket of tea leaves she has gathered in the afternoon and walks back to the farmhouse.

Jeena walks behind her silently. Indhu knows saying goodbye will be hard, but it must be done. They return to the change room, bathe and drape their sarees across their aching, tired bodies. As they pin each other's pleated pallus to the back of their saree blouses, Jeena tentatively asks, "Will you email me Indhu?"

"Of course Jeena. You don't need to ask, you should know that I will email you as often as I can."

They walk out towards the entrance of the tea plantation. Indhu catches sight of Prasoon's Royal Enfield motorcycle parked a few metres away from the plantation. As they approach him, Jeena tightly grips Indhu's hand.

"Are you sure this is what you want Indhu? You know your father will never take you back once you leave."

"I know Jeena, but how else will I be happy? Prasoon. Prasoon, he is all the stars in my night sky, he is my Sun. We cannot live without the Sun you know Jeena. And I cannot live without him. I don't want to do this - I need to, *priyappetta*. It's hard to leave *amma* (mother) and *aniyan* (younger brother), but I know they will be well. *Aniyan* will forget me soon, he is too young. It's better if he forgets."

They look at each other for a long while. Indhu takes in everything of Jeena - the perfectly round face, the olive tone of her freckled skin, her wavy black hair, her almond-shaped eyes, her rosy cheeks. The memory of her best friend's beauty is an image that will undoubtedly comfort her in times of loneliness and despair.

Indhu gently strokes Jeena's cheek. "*Vandanam varam priyappetta* (may peace be with you dear)."

She brushes away the fresh stream of tears on Jeena's cheeks and whispers in her ear the first line from a sacred Hindu prayer they have recited together so many times while working in the tea fields. "*Sarvesham svastir bhava-tu* (may auspiciousness be unto all)."

Indhu kisses her friend one last time on the cheek and pulls away from her gently. "*Vita priyappetta* (fare-well dear)."

She tentatively lets go of Jeena's trembling hand and walks briskly to Prasoon. He takes her tenderly by the hand and helps her onto the motorcycle. As he starts the engine, she turns and looks back at Jeena. Her face is tear stained but she is smiling broadly at Indhu and vigorously waving.

"*Nannayi peayi* (go well) Indhu!"

As Prasoon accelerates Indhu turns to hold him around the waist. She buries her head in his jacket and cries unreservedly. She cries because she knows that she willingly leaves behind her sweet friend; she willingly leaves behind her loving mother and younger brother; she willingly leaves behind the pristine tea fields, the picturesque rolling hills and the peaceful valleys of her hometown; she willingly leaves behind the untold beauty of Munnar.

But despite all her tears, Indhu knows that the love of her best friend Jeena, her mother and brother, and the infinite beauty of Munnar will forever live within her heart.

Tears in Munnar (Part 2)

"It is such a secret place, the land of tears"

ANTOINE DE SAINT-EXUPERY

Jeena picks up the last basket of tea leaves and walks slowly towards the factory. The Kanan Devan Hills Plantation has been her source of freedom and joy, a respite from the endless troubles of her home. Her lower back aches and her swollen feet slow her down. Her rounded belly is heavy and tires her but she pushes on.

As the day draws to a close, she is grateful that the baby has decided not to come today. Exhausted and hungry, she bathes, changes into her clean saree and starts the long walk home. She is eager to see the children. Suraya is three, walking and talking as if the world is at her fingertips, waiting to be explored. Aru is one, learning to walk, constantly babbling an indecipherable language and excessively doting on his sister. They are her pride and joy, the reason she is alive. If it were not for her babies, she would have taken her own life a long time ago.

There is only one thing she does not look forward to when going home. Seeing Aditya. Aditya is everything a husband should not be. Callous. Cold. Angry. Abusive. He has never shown her an inch of love or affection. Heartless from day one, he's brutally beaten, bruised and battered her. He's kicked her in the head, in the chest, in the abdomen even when pregnant with Aru. And still she has no choice but to stay with him.

She could never go back to her parents even if she wanted to. She's made her bed and now she has to lie in it - her parents would never take her back into their lives. Once a girl leaves her home, her family, she cannot return - she belongs to her husband. She shudders at the thought of lying next to him every night for the rest of her life - helpless and at his merciless disposal. She is nothing but an object to him - a toy he plays with at his whim and fancy, thoughtlessly taking her dignity, humiliating her and she has no choice but to give in like a puppet on strings, with no control of her own life or destiny.

Jeena walks into the house. She hears the laughter of Suraya and Aru in the next room. Carefree as ever. She walks into their room and they scream with joy at the sight of their mother. She bends towards them and embraces them tightly, holding them close to her bosom. Suraya pulls away and whispers in her ear, "*Amma, appa,* is here."

"Okay, Suraya. Look after your brother. I will go cook supper."

She walks into the kitchen. Aditya sits at the kitchen table with a half full bottle of toddy next to him. He's been drinking when he should be at work. She greets him softly. He turns and looks at her with a smirk across his face.

"My beautiful Jeena. Where have you been all afternoon? Where is my supper?"

"Aditya, I was at work. They gave me the afternoon shift today at the plantation. I will prepare your supper now."

"I don't care! My supper should be ready by now! You whore! How do I know if you were really at work? You could be earning your wage with other men! How would I know?"

He leaps from his chair and hits her across her cheek. He kicks her in the abdomen and pushes her to the floor. She moans in pain but it doesn't stop him. He kicks her repeatedly in her stomach and pushes her head against the wall. Her head starts bleeding but she is helpless, defenseless. She tries not to cry out too loud, fearing that she will attract the attention of the children.

Eventually he tires out and stops the abuse. He walks out of the kitchen, into the garden. Jeena lies lifelessly on the kitchen floor. The pain in her stomach is excruciating. Silent tears fall down her cheeks. She fears that the unborn child may not survive. She soon realizes that she is bleeding profusely. Her saree is wet with a growing pool of deep red blood spreading around her thighs. She whimpers, not from the physical pain but from the heartache and sorrow. She knows she has lost the unborn baby.

Jeena lies on the floor in the pool of blood for a while. It's as if time doesn't pass. She's delirious. Her face is pale, she has no strength to lift herself up. She knows Aditya has left. He's gone to the nearest toddy bar to drink himself into oblivion once more. In the distance, she hears women's voices. She calls out to them. Again, and again she calls.

Eventually the women hear and come towards the house. As they near she recognizes the voice of one woman - Indhu's mother. Relief washes over her, she knows she will be well looked after with Indhu's mother.

As they approach the kitchen door, she cries out in agony and reaches out to them. The tears flow without reservation. She couldn't care if her children see her anguish. The women gasp at the sight of her on the floor. They act immediately as only mothers can - they lift her from the floor, wipe away and clean the blood off the floor, rip her saree and underskirt off her thin frame, wash her in the bathroom and dry her tears. A neighbour watches over the children.

The women take great care when handling the still-born baby. Once Jeena is bathed and in a clean saree, she comes into the kitchen and reaches out for her stillborn child. The tears stream silently down her cheeks. They wrap the child in white calico cloth. The women know that the baby cannot be cremated unless the father is present - it would be futile to summon the priest now. Indhu's mother sends word with her son to pass the message to Aditya. But they all know he will not come - by now he will be oblivious to anything but his own drunken desires - his addiction consumes him.

The women feed the children and put them to sleep. They coax some food into Jeena's mouth - trying to en-courage her to eat for the sake of her young ones. It is 9 o'clock when they leave Jeena alone with her children in her house, alone with her sorrow and pain, alone with the lifeless body of her stillborn child.

***

The next morning Jeena wakes to find Aditya lying next to her. The baby wrapped in calico is in a reed basket by her bedside. She cannot gather enough strength to lift herself from the bed. Eventually she gets up and slowly walks to the children's bedroom. They're still sound asleep. She bathes herself and starts to prepare breakfast.

As she stands at the stove preparing the morning's dosa and sambal she contemplates the possibility of killing Aditya. It is not the first time that the menacing thought has crossed her mind. For the past two years, every time Aditya has laid his hand on her, the thought of ending his life has predominated her thoughts, becoming stronger with every agonizing strike against her body. Why should she have to endure this pain, this callous abuse? Surely this cannot be what is preordained for her? Surely, she deserves better? Jeena has considered the many ways that she could kill Aditya. Poisoning his food. Stabbing him whilst asleep. Pushing him over the mountainside. Or simply shooting him at point-blank range in their home with his own gun.

She jerks out of her dark thoughts. Aditya wakes whilst she is in the kitchen. He wobbles into the kitchen, clearly hung over from the night before. The children play outside in the morning sunshine.

He abruptly asks, "What happened last night? Where is the baby?"

Jeena feebly responds, "After you kicked me in the stomach, I had a miscarriage."

"So, you're blaming the child's death on me? You piece of..."

Before he completes his slanderous sentence, he pushes her to the floor and kicks her in the stomach over and over again until he exhausts himself. She takes the battering wordlessly. Not a cry or moan of pain escapes her lips.

Jeena has become physically and psychologically numb to her husband's ruthless abuse.

While Jeena lies on the floor, attempting to recover from the beating, Aditya helps himself to breakfast. After much effort, Jeena lifts herself off the ground and leans against the stove.

Despite the difficulty in catching her breath, she says the necessary words. "We need to cremate the child, Aditya."

He grunts as he fills his mouth with a handful of dosa and sambal. His indecipherable response leaves Jeena wondering how the man could be so emotionless at a time like this.

Aditya summons the local priest to preside over the cremation of the stillborn baby. The child's ashes are placed in an urn. Aditya and Jeena accompany the priest to release the ashes into the Nallathanni River. Jeena watches as the ashes meet the water. Tears stream down her pale cheeks. Aditya turns, leaves her by the riverbank and walks to the nearest toddy bar. Once again, she is left alone with her heartache and grief.

***

Days and weeks pass by. Life continues in Munnar as it always has. Jeena spends her days at the tea plantation earning the sole income for their household. Aditya spends his time (and Jeena's money) at toddy bars. And of course, whenever he is enraged by some supposed shortcoming of Jeena's he lashes out at her, beats her until she's black and blue. But Jeena does not defend her-self, she takes the beating every time as if she deserves it, as if she has become numb and feels nothing. Killing Aditya is a thought that increasingly floods most of her waking hours.

One day as she returns home from the tea plantation, she sees a woman standing in her garden, engaging so lovingly with the children as they play. As she nears the house, she realizes that this is no stranger. Her slender figure and long black hair haven't changed since Jeena last saw her five years ago.

"Indhu? Is that you?"

The woman turns and for sure, the crinkling frown lines and the dark circles under her eyes are still there. But she smiles as if she has not a care in the world. So unlike Indhu.

"Jeena! My friend!"

They run to each other and tightly embrace. Soon enough there are tears streaming down Jeena's face. But for once these are tears of joy.

"Indhu what are you doing here in Munnar? Where's Prasoon?"

"I came to visit my family, to visit you *priyappetta* (dear). Prasoon is with his parents now. They are so happy to see him. My parents too are so happy to see me. They've forgiven me for marrying Prasoon and eloping with him five years ago. Tell me Jeena, how have you been? My mother told me what happened with your last pregnancy. How are you now *priyappetta*?"

Indhu asks the question and strokes Jeena's cheek at the same time. Jeena succumbs to the tears that have been welling up inside her. She cries her heart out knowing that for once there is someone to comfort her, to listen, to dry her tears.

Indhu takes her inside and they sit at the kitchen table. The children play in their room. Jeena tells Indhu everything - how she was married to Aditya to pay off her father's debt to him; how he has raped her from the very first night of marriage; how she has no choice but to give in to his every whim and fancy; how he kicks and beats her until he's exhausted whenever he is enraged by some shortcoming of hers. She cries without reservation as she tells Indhu the story of her life.

"*Priyappetta*, why do you stay? Why not leave him, run away? You could come to Cochin, stay with us for a while. Why do you just accept all this abuse? You and your children deserve better Jeena."

"I can't leave Indhu, he will come looking for me. He will kill me if I leave."

"Have you laid a complaint with the police?"

"The police? Please Indhu you should know what they are like here in Munnar. They would take the husband's side for sure. They would never defend or protect a woman."

"Have you ever tried to defend yourself?"

"Indhu if I defend myself he will only beat me more. If I resist or hit him back, he will beat harder, he will even try to kill me. I mean nothing to him."

As she says the last sentence she bursts into tears again and holds onto Indhu's hands tightly.

"Jeena I have a plan. I cannot see you suffer anymore. Does Aditya have a gun?"

"What? Yes, he does but what are you thinking Indhu? We cannot risk doing anything foolish. This is my karma and I have to live with it."

She is burdened by her dark thoughts and is desperate to tell Indhu, but she is too ashamed.

"No, I will not see you live like this! You deserve better *priyapppetta!*"

Indhu explains her plan to Jeena. Jeena listens but knows in her heart that she cannot do it, despite all her premeditations.

She suddenly realizes that she has not asked Indhu about her life with Prasoon, about life in Cochin.

"Indhu, what about you? How is life in Cochin? How is life with Prasoon?"

"Jeena, I couldn't have asked for a better husband. That's why I cannot see you suffer at the hands of Aditya. He is a monster. Prasoon loves and respects me unconditionally, he treats me like a piece of gold and to think I haven't given him any children. We have tried for so long, but my womb is barren. We are considering going to a fertility clinic when we return to Cochin. I want to be a mother like you. But fate it seems doesn't want me to. So, I'm going to defy fate and try to become a mother."

The friends smile at each other lovingly. Indhu tells Jeena to think about the plan she has devised. She leaves and Jeena begins to prepare supper for her deranged husband.

***

The next day Indhu goes to Jeena's house at dusk to see what she has decided. Jeena looks like she hasn't slept the night before. She looks tired and drained.

"Jeena what have you decided *priyapppetta?*"

Jeena trembles as she responds. She is no murderer, but what choice does she have?

"Indhu I will do it. But promise me something. Promise me that if anything happens to me, you will take my children and look after them - I don't want them to be orphans living here in Munnar. Promise me Indhu that you'll give them a better life. Please don't send the children to my parents. They don't even know I have children. They have gone to Thekkady. My father has run away from all the people he owes money to here in Munnar. Knowing him he'll try to sell my children in Thekkady in exchange for reducing his new debts. Promise me you will take them!"

"Of course I will Jeena. But why are you thinking this?"

"I've even written it in my will, Indhu. No one can go against this. Look. I don't know if everything will go according to plan, Indhu. What if they take me to jail? Or what if he uses the same gun to kill me? What of my children? Promise me you'll look after them, Indhu."

"Yes, yes, I will look after them as if they were my own. Do not worry Jeena. But please don't think these thoughts."

She embraces Jeena and wipes away her tears.

***

When Jeena is alone in the kitchen preparing supper for Aditya, she runs through the plan in her head one last time. The gun is in the cupboard under the sink. She will grab it as he eats. The children will be asleep. In his drunken stupour he won't be able to defend himself as she kills him.

As the plan runs through her mind, Aditya returns home.

He grunts a greeting to her and sits at the table waiting to be served. She serves him the paratha and the curries she's made. Her ongoing premeditations have come to life. She reassures herself that killing him is a matter of survival or else she will inevitably lose her sanity or worse yet, die at the hands of her merciless husband.

Slowly she turns and reaches into the cupboard. Her hands are trembling. Her fingers find the gun. She swings around. She doesn't aim, her fingers fumble for the trigger.

The silence is shattered by a massive bang.

Blood gushes from Aditya's head. But he is alive.

Horror etched across his face, he leaps towards Jeena and seizes her by the throat.

Whatever life is left in him he uses to squeeze at her throat, wringing Jeena's neck. She has no space to breathe, let alone utter a word.

The silent suffering of her life stays with her in death.

Images of her beautiful children flash across her wide eyes before silence envelops her. Aditya emits a horrible, guttural sound in the last, furious throes of life.

He watches his wife's body slump to the floor before he gasps his last breath and collapses on the kitchen floor beside her. The lifeless bodies are unremarkable but for the fact that their faces, etched in pain, look away from one another.

***

Indhu hears the gunshot in the distance. She looks at Prasoon standing next to her in her mother's kitchen.

"That's Jeena. She's done it. I need to go to her. Come with me, Prasoon. We need to help her get on the next bus to Cochin before the police go to the house."

They arrive at Jeena's house. Indhu races inside and stops short in the kitchen. She stares at the sight before her.

"Oh God! Jeena! Jeena! Wake up *priyapppetta*! Please Jeena wake up! You can't leave your babies alone Jeena! Wake up!"

Indhu is in tears. She pats Jeena on the cheeks and shakes her, trying desperately to wake her up. Prasoon bends down and holds her. He notices the inflamed bruises around Jeena's pale neck.

"Indhu, she's gone. We need to call the police. He strangled her."

"The children. What will happen to them? She said I should look after them if anything were to happen to her. This was not meant to happen, Prasoon. She can't just leave her children to us. She's their mother!"

"Indhu, she chose you to raise her children - you have to respect her wishes. They have no one else."

Prasoon embraces her and brushes away her tears.

***

Soon the police arrive. They take a statement from Prasoon and Jeena as they are the first people to arrive at the crime scene. The children cry when they are woken up and see their parents dead on the kitchen floor. Indhu tries her best to comfort them, they bury their heads in the folds of her saree and hold on to her neck tightly.

The police inspector approaches Indhu.

"Ms. Mudaly, do you know if your friend has a will?"

"Yes, inspector she has a will."

She turns to the drawer behind her and pulls out the will from underneath the tablecloth and kitchen towels. She hands it over to the inspector. He unfolds it and reads it silently.

"Ms. Mudaly it would seem that she has chosen you to be the legal guardian of the children. Do you accept this responsibility? If you do, you will need to accompany me to the station so that you can fill out the adoption papers."

"Yes, I accept. They are my children from now onwards."

Indhu is in tears but she holds the young children close to her bosom. They are all she has of Jeena now, and she and Prasoon are all they have.

***

Two days later, Indhu and Prasoon lock the simple house once owned by Jeena and Aditya. Each of them carries a child. They've packed the children's clothes and their few belongings.

Before they leave Munnar they stop at the Nallathanni River and release Jeena and Aditya's ashes into the water. The children cry - Suraya knows she will never see her parents again. Aru is too young to understand what has happened, he just imitates the behaviour of his sister.

Indhu, Prasoon and the children take the next bus back to Cochin. Throughout the journey home, Indhu thinks how strange it is that fate never wanted her to know the joy of giving birth to her own children.

Now she knows why. Fate knew that she would one day be bestowed the responsibility of her best friend's children. Fate knew she would one day be a mother, not to her own biological children, but to the two innocent or-phaned children of Jeena. The thought that her beautiful Jeena is no more brings Indhu to tears.

She cries herself to sleep, leaning on the shoulder of Prasoon. And as they leave behind the peaceful green hills of Munnar, Indhu hopes they will leave behind all the tears and heartache too. She knows that even though they leave Munnar behind, the memory of Jeena will live forever in her heart, and the hearts of her young children.

Forbidden love in Kovalam

"For all its accolades and celebrated recognition as sound guidance, I have personally noticed that sometimes, 'follow your heart', is really bad advice"

STEVE MARABOLI

Shobana neatens the pleats on her silk saree. She fidgets nervously in the kitchen waiting to be called into the sitting room. She has done this so many times. No matter how handsome or highly educated the boy is, her mother is never happy. And her father? He just submits to her mother's wishes. If the boy is not good enough for Jayalakshmi, then he is not good enough for Balachandran either. That's the way things go in the Shunmugam household.

"Shobana, come my dear."

Her mother summons her. She stands and neatens the cerise saree one last time. She checks her reflection in the mirror alongside the kitchen door. The jasmine flowers in her hair are perfectly in place, falling from her bun. Her jewels sparkle in the afternoon sunlight streaming through the window. She walks to the sitting room and nervously greets the boy's family.

She takes her seat next to her mother and looks timidly at the floor. She knows that she cannot make eye contact with any of the guests unless they speak to her, and she may certainly not have a passing glance at the boy.

"Shobana is a chartered accountant. She started a new job as a junior accountant at an international accounting firm three months ago. We like our daughters to be independent and strong working women."

Her father usually begins by boasting about his daughter's qualification.

"It is excellent for a young woman to be educated and working these days, Bala. You must be so proud. Our Anirudh is a senior actuary - he has made us so proud. It is wonderful to see our children soar to greater heights than us."

"Indeed. So Anirudh is looking to settle down, Gopi?"

"Yes Bala. He is looking for a good girl, educated and working. Your beautiful Shobana here would be a perfect match for him. He doesn't believe an educated woman should stay at home and waste her talent and skill."

"That is rare in young men these days, Gopi. Okay, well we have the birth dates - we will consult our priest and contact you thereafter. Thank you for coming over. May we have good news for you the next time I call."

"Thank you Bala for considering our son. Your daughter would be well looked after in our family. Please remember that."

As everyone stands to say goodbye, Shobana tentatively raises her light brown eyes off the floor and gives Anirudh a quick glance. So handsome! As she lets her gaze fall back to the floor, she catches Anirudh as he furtively glances at her. Shobana finds herself blushing.

The families bid farewell to one another and as her father closes the front door, her mother lets out a sigh.

"No. No. No. He is not right for my daughter. I do not believe a single word his father has said about an educated girl not staying at home and wasting her talent. Liar!"

"But Jaya you can see they are good Hindu people. The boy's own mother still works to this day! What more do you want for our Shobana - he is handsome, highly educated and promises to take good care of her, and she can still work!"

"Bala, I will not waste my time taking the birthdates to the priest. I have made my decision. She will not marry such a boy! It does not feel right, I feel it in my bones!"

"But Jaya have you not considered what Shobana may want? Sometimes I think you just don't want to let go of her, our last unmarried child. But she's getting older Jaya, she needs to find a husband soon!"

"I want to get her married as much as you do Bala! But to the right person. This one is no good for my Shobana."

Her parents continue to bicker over the latest suitor. Shobana quietly walks up the stairs to her room and closes the door behind her. She pulls the flowers from her hair, pulls the bangles off her wrists and collapses onto her bed in tears. For once this boy Anirudh felt like he could have been the one but as expected, he was not good enough for her mother, just like the countless boys before him.

***

Shobana cries herself to sleep and wakes when the sun filters through her curtains and falls quietly across her face. The rough silk saree has left crease lines on her cheek.

It is 6am in Kovalam. She hurriedly bathes and dresses for work. Another day as a junior accountant at the firm. Another day to blindly search for her soul mate, for a potential husband, for a future other than the one slowly panning out in her parents' home as a spinster.

She walks into the office and takes her seat at her desk. It's the usual. Email requests from her manager to audit the books of five new companies. She schedules appointments with these companies and then looks at the last bit of auditing of the previous companies she was tasked with.

***

It's 2:15pm and the financial manager from one of the new companies is late for their appointment. Shobana taps her pencil on the desk in the boardroom impatiently. She cannot afford to run late. At 2:20pm she hears someone enter at reception. In a few seconds he is escorted by the receptionist to the boardroom. Shobana stands and neatens the pleats of her saree. An obsessive habit she's had since a teenager.

She raises her head to greet the client. As her eyes fall to his face, she is taken aback, mesmerized by his green eyes, his handsome smile.

"Good afternoon Ms. Shunmugam. I am Shafi Khan, financial manager of Mallika Silks. How do you do? My apologies for arriving so late. Traffic."

"Good. Good afternoon Mr. Khan. No it's no problem. I'm. I'm well thank you and how are you? Please have a seat."

Shobana feels her heart beat so rapidly she knows he can probably hear it pound loudly in her chest. She has never felt like this before. Her mind goes blank and she forces herself to focus on the agenda she has put together for this meeting.

Eventually, the introductory meeting is over, a timeline is set for the audits to be conducted at Mallika Silks by herself and her team. Shafi and Shobana shake hands and say goodbye.

Shobana drops her papers at her desk and hurries to the restroom. She splashes cold water on her face and tells herself to get a grip. Fancying a Muslim would get her nowhere. She is a Hindu and a Hindu she must marry. She dabs her face with a paper towel and returns to her desk.

***

Over the next few days the audits begin at all the new clients. Shobana divides her team such that she is always the assigned auditor at Mallika Silks. She knows she should not be doing this. But she feels compelled to.

She sees Shafi almost every day of the week. He smiles sweetly at her. She notices that he wears no wedding ring. They exchange pleasantries and converse briefly about the audit. One day towards the end of Shobana's shift he asks her out for coffee. Shobana, never before asked out by any male, stares at him with her mouth agape.

She slowly begins to stutter, "Shafi, I. I - I have to be home by - by 5:30 to help my mother with - with dinner. I'm - I'm sorry. Maybe - maybe next time?"

Before Shafi can even think of a response Shobana is out the door. She is breathless when she gets onto the bus. Her heart pounds in her chest, she can hear it thumping vigorously in her ears. She cannot allow this to happen. He cannot fall for her just as she cannot allow herself to fall for him.

***

The audit at Mallika Silks draws to a conclusion. The report is due to be submitted by Shobana in a few hours. She hurriedly signs off on the document, makes a copy for her file and catches the train to Mallika's head office to meet Shafi.

When she arrives, she is taken to his office by the receptionist. He smiles broadly when he sees her. She tentatively smiles back. They discuss the audit for a while and she hands over the audit report to him. As she gives it to him, his fingers brush against hers. She feels a tingling sensation in her hand, and perhaps her heart.

He reads through the report briefly, asks a few questions and then closes it.

Without looking at her he says, "Shobana. I have watched you over the past three weeks. I'd be lying if I said that you have not caught my eye. I have never seen anyone more beautiful than you. You have a beautiful soul. I know that you feel something when we are together just as I do. I see it in your eyes when you look at me. Can I please take you out for coffee? I would love to get to know you more. I know you are hesitant, you have never been asked out by a male have you? I can see you are a good girl. But one cup of coffee is harmless. Please."

"Shafi, I have never gone out with a male before, you are right. But I am Hindu, you are Muslim. Where would a single cup of coffee lead us both? Nowhere."

She looks away and holds back the tears. She wants to so desperately say yes to the coffee date but she wouldn't be able to live with herself if she says yes to him.

"Shobana, tell me, you are old enough to be married, but why aren't you?"

"Shafi. Shafi, you wouldn't understand. My mother."

Before she can complete her sentence Shobana bursts into tears. Shafi gets up and comes around to her, he pulls out his handkerchief and wipes the tears from her face.

"Shobana, sweet Shobana. Please, as friends, let's go for coffee and you can tell me what saddens you so."

She looks at Shafi. No one has ever shown her such tenderness before. She gives in. After all what can a harmless cup of coffee between two colleagues, two friends do?

"Okay. Just one cup of coffee."

They have coffee at a nearby cafe. Shobana spills her heart out to Shafi. She tells him how no boy is ever good enough for her mother, how her father just gives in to her. She tells him how she fears that she'll die a spinster having spent her whole life living with her parents, never knowing the joy of love.

He tries to comfort her. Without hesitating he wipes away her tears and gently holds her hand as she weeps. Shobana knows that this should not be happening. But she doesn't pull away. She allows him to comfort her, to hold her hand so tenderly.

As dusk approaches, they say goodbye and go their separate ways. He watches her walk into the distance and feels his heart desire something he knows is forbidden.

His family would never accept her unless she converts to Islam. But why have his thoughts gone that far?

Shobana cannot stop thinking about Shafi. He consumes her every waking thought. At work she is distracted. At home she stares blankly out the window at the passing cars. Her parents can barely extract 10 words from her. She knows that Shafi is the pulse she feels within her heart, the reason she is alive. But how can she yearn so deeply for someone who is forbidden to her as a Hindu? How can she feel such intense love for him, when this love is taboo?

***

A week later, Shafi decides to call her at the office. She takes his call, ecstatic to hear his soft, soothing voice. He asks her if they can meet for coffee again. Without hesitating she says yes.

And so their clandestine relationship begins. A coffee date every second day. A brief moment when they hold hands, when he caresses her cheek. A fleeting moment when they exchange a smile only lovers would exchange.

***

Four months after their first date, Shafi plucks up the courage to ask Shobana if she would convert to Islam so that they can marry. He knows she is a devout Hindu, as are her parents. He knows it will be difficult for her to respond.

Shobana looks at him emotionlessly. Suddenly her eyes glaze over and tears fall across her pale cheeks.

"Shafi I would do anything to be with you, to be your wife. But asking me to no longer be a Hindu, I don't know if I can ever do that."

"It's okay Shobana. Why don't you think about it?"

***

Shobana spends many sleepless nights thinking about Shafi's proposition. She now knows he wishes to marry her. But the only way is for her to convert to Islam. It would break her parents to know their youngest child had chosen to become a Muslim.

She knows that their priest forbids Hindus to convert to any religion. He always says, "You are born a Hindu, you will die a Hindu. Converting to other religions means nothing, you will always be a Hindu, even in the next life."

Perhaps that sentiment consoles Shobana. She may convert to Islam, practice Islam, change her name but she will always be a Hindu even in the next life. Shafi probably does not know of such a notion. Perhaps it's better for him to not know. So maybe converting to Islam is not such a taboo - after all she will be a Hindu in heart and soul until the day she dies, even in the next life - Islam will not be able to take the "Hindu" out of her. She finds comfort in that thought.

***

Shobana tells Shafi of her decision. She will convert to Islam to be with him. If she loves Shafi like the Earth loves the Sun, into eternity, then she will do anything to be with him. Shafi tells her he will come with his parents to ask her family for her hand in marriage.

Soon enough the day arrives when Shafi and his parents are due to visit Shobana's parents. Shobana fidgets nervously in her room. What will her parents think? What will they say? They will be angry for sure.

As 12 o'clock approaches Shobana neatens the pleats of her sapphire blue saree. She goes downstairs and tells her parents that some people will be coming to visit. Her mother sees the flowers in her hair and the bangles on her wrists.

"Shobana is it a boy? Is his family coming to ask for your hand?"

"Yes. It is a boy. I met him through my work. He is gentle and kind."

Her father winks at her. "Shobana, for your sake I hope he ticks all your mother's boxes."

"Don't joke Bala. I think Shobana is finally tired of me making choices for her. About time she chooses someone for herself. Good girl Shobana. I've been waiting for this day, for you to bring home the boy you've fallen in love with. Arranged marriages are never good - look at your father and I, we are forever bickering."

With that all three of them burst into laughter.

But Shobana's laughter is coloured with shades of apprehension and nervousness. She cannot stop fidgeting. Soon enough there is a knock on the door and her mother chases her into the kitchen.

She listens as her father greets the guests and invites them in. She hears her mother softly gasp as she takes in the fact that her guests are Muslim.

Pleasantries are exchanged. Eventually they turn to the main reason for their visit. Shafi's father asks for Shobana's hand in marriage to their son.

Shobana's father is silent, dumbstruck perhaps. Shobana's mother on the other hand lets out a piercing scream and shouts, "Never! Never will a child of my womb marry a Muslim! Never! How can my Shobana do this to me! Get out of my house! Get out!"

The guests rush out of the house, mumbling to each other in disdain. Shobana feels herself collapse to the floor. Tears stream down her cheeks. She feels herself turn numb. Her enraged mother storms into the kitchen and slaps her across the face.

"How can you do this to me? To your father? After all we have given you, this is how you say thanks? You ungrateful imbecile! Have you no common sense? We are born Hindus - we will die Hindus! And yet you bring home a Muslim boy? Are you mad?"

She kicks Shobana in the abdomen thrice and slaps her repeatedly across her face. Shobana does not say a word. She silently takes the beating from her mother, tears falling quietly across her face. Her father eventually comes and pulls her mother away from her. Her parents struggle for a few minutes until her mother calms down. Her father helps Shobana to her feet and sends her to her room.

Shobana obliviously unties her saree and changes into a nightdress. She lies lifelessly on her bed and cries silently. She eventually falls asleep on a damp pillow.

***

In the morning she dresses for work and leaves home without saying a word to her parents. Her stomach grumbles - she has not eaten since yesterday morning. But she couldn't care less. She has no appetite. Life suddenly has no meaning now that she knows Shafi cannot be hers and she cannot be Shafi's. Her soul is shattered, broken.

She decides to walk to work today. The scorching Kovalam sun hits her face but she does not notice. She reaches the bridge that she must cross to get to town. As she begins the long walk across the bridge, she realizes how unjust life can be.

The priest had said countless times before that if you're born a Hindu you will die a Hindu. Converting to Islam would just be a necessary rite to enter Shafi's home and family. Despite her conversion, despite her new name and new way of life she would always be a Hindu. What was the problem? Why could her mother not allow her daughter to be happy just once?

She stares at the water in the river below. So calm, so serene, so unlike the raging storm brewing within her. With the little strength she has, she lifts herself up onto the wooden railing of the bridge and stands up, struggling to keep her balance.

Before any pedestrian or driver notices, Shobana lets herself fall freely, gracefully into the deep water below, drowning her beautiful spirit, drowning her heartache and pain, drowning her forbidden love.

Note:

This story is dedicated to individuals who are not allowed the opportunity to 'follow their hearts' because boundaries of religion and faith cannot be crossed in the name of love.

POETRY

"Dear one, there is a way from your
heart to my heart,
And there is an awareness in my heart
because of seeking it,
Because my heart is like pure sweet water,
And pure water holds the mirror for
the moon"

— JALAL AL-DIN RUMI
FROM DIVAN-E SHAMS-E TABRIZI: QUATRAIN 334

MY ETERNAL SUN,
MY ETERNAL MOON

Who will be my eternal Sun, my eternal Moon?
He will be the gentle wind lifting my sails
He will be my song on repeat, my happy tune
He will be the remedy I turn to when all else fails.

Who will be my eternal Sun, my eternal Moon?
He will be my rainbow after the rain
He will be a blessing, my destined boon
He will be the oxygen that runs through my every vein.

Who will be my eternal Sun, my eternal Moon?
He will be the dawn at the end of my dark night
He will calm my fears, his words will be my cocoon
He will be the lone candle that brings me light.

Who will be my eternal Sun, my eternal Moon?
He will sweeten the honey from the bee
He will be the beauty of a new springtime bloom
He will be the stable roots and I, the restless tree.

Who will be my eternal Sun, my eternal Moon?
He will be the pretty petals of my lilac rose
He will be the balm that heals my wound
I will be the lyrical poem and he, my unpolished prose.

Who will be my eternal Sun, my eternal Moon?
He will be the countless stars in my indigo sky
He will be the vast ocean in its every hue
He will be the tear of joy that falls from my eye.

Who will be my eternal Sun, my eternal Moon?
He will be the sweet song that lulls me to sleep.
If he is mine, he will come to me soon
For he is the pulse I feel within me so deep -
He will be my eternal Sun, my eternal Moon.

YOUR FOOTPRINTS ON MY HEART
(PART 1)

Thank you for the footprints you've left on my heart
I know I will never be the same
You've left a little part of you in me, a piece of your heart
And I hope these footprints never wane.

Thank you for the footprints you've left on my soul
I have a fraction of your joy, your wisdom, your pain
It is these gentle footprints that make me whole
For it is your friendship that no words can explain.

Thank you for the footprints you've left on my heart
I hope they will live within me 'til the day I die
For you piece me together when I fall apart
For you give me my sunshine and the blue of my sky.

A SONNET FOR LAKE VEMBANAD

The waters flow calmly before me, so blue -
The Cormorant ducks paddle, dive below,
They surface with shiny fish, hard earned jewels,
The houseboat floats gently, ever so slow.

The waters of Lake Vembanad mesmerize -
I absorb the beauty of my Motherland,
I feel stillness and peace within me rise,
And I reflect on my roots, my homeland.

The waters glisten in the glorious sun,
I see people bathe in the backwaters,
I hear the Keralan deckhand softly hum,
I am silenced by the radiant waters.

Lake Vembanad quietens my restless soul,
Its beauty fills my heart and makes me whole.

LITTLE BIRD

Little bird, you sing sweetly by my window -
Do you bring me a message from above?
Little bird, your song takes away my sorrow,
And your melody fills my heart with love.

Little bird, oh handsome one, why have you come?
Your tune leaves footprints on my heart,
You comfort me like the warmth of the sun,
But little bird why have you entered my heart?

Little bird, you are here for no reason known to you and I,
You come and go - your absence leaves me yearning.
Why are you here little bird, flying softly in my blue sky?
You're here now, so the fire in my heart is burning.

Little bird, why do you grace my lonely indigo skies?
Your mysterious presence brings peace to my soul,
But little bird you depart now, and endless tears fill my eyes,
For your sweet song once made my heart whole.

DON'T BE AFRAID

Dear one, in your moments of despair, don't be afraid
Know that on this path you are not alone
You travel with constant companions
Who can so gently guide you home
Their wisdom uplifts and their kindness does not fade.

In your moments of deep loss, heartache and sorrow
Know that there are some who will not leave your side
You have beacons of light every step of the way
Who provide a listening ear when you need to confide
And may lead you to the unknown beauties of tomorrow.

In your moments of inner turmoil, confusion and pain
Know that joyful memories live within you, a joyful future too
Your story is unfolding, the pages are turning
Your heart holds the footprints of
those who truly love you -
They are the bright suns that hide behind the rain.

IF YOU GIVE ME THE TWILIGHT SKY

If you give me the twilight sky,
I'll give you the stars above.
If you give me a blank canvas,
I'll give you beautiful art.
If you give me yours,
I'll give you my undying love -
I'll give you my every breath,
I'll give you my whole heart.

If you give me the twilight sky,
I'll give you the sun and moon.
If you give me blank paper,
I'll give you poetry from my soul.
If you give me your heart,
I'll give you mine too -
I'll give you all of me, my every cell,
for you make me whole.

If you give me the twilight sky,
I'll give you the Milky Way.
If you become a mirror to my soul,
I will become a mirror to yours.
If you hold my hand and walk beside me,
I will let you stay -
For you will be the one and only
who walks to my midnight shores.

IF THE BIRDS STOP SINGING

If Man were to live foolishly and without care,
We would be without flourishing fields,
without the blue of our sky,
And if the birds stop singing, would it
be something Man could bear?
For there will be silence, deep silence that darkens the sky.

If the sparrow tweets no more, and the
wagtail does not bob around,
Would life be the same for you, for me?
If no swallows soar ahead, and the
lark's call is an unknown sound,
What would life become for you, for me?

Does the song of the bird touch your soul, touch your heart?
Would you hurt, despair or mourn if the
birds no longer sweetly sing?
Without the honeyed song of the bird,
life itself would fall apart,
For it's the pulse of nature, every tweet
and chirrup, every song they sing.

If the mother goose no longer calls and
the grey dove no longer coos,
Would your life and mine be the same?

If there is an end to the weaver's twitter
and the owl's night-time ruse,
Would life still be bright and be much the same?

No. If the birds stop singing, a dark
silence would surely fill the air,
Life would not be the same, we would
yearn for the lost song.
If the birds stop singing, nature would
be lonesome and bare,
For the skies and the depths of our ears
are where the sweet birds belong.

If the birds stop singing, we will have
quiet winds and lonely trees,
For the skies and the depths of our ears are
where the songs of birds should be.

THE OLD TURKISH LADY

The crisp, clear mountain air awakens me
There is natural beauty all around - I'm in awe,
The people are warm, content and perhaps carefree
I am surrounded by the charm of southern Turkey.

We slowly return to the bus, but we pause
A lady with a white headscarf sitting
at the corner beckons
She cannot speak our language,
Yet she gestures lovingly for me to sit next to her.

She is wrinkled beyond measure, but she smiles
broadly, sincerely –
Her wrinkles move gracefully, as if
familiar with the form of her smile
She gives me a dry kiss upon my cheek
and I feel a shiver down my spine.

The old Turkish lady reaching out to me has become a
dear memory,
Her unrestrained warmth reminds me that
love is beyond geographical boundaries,
Beyond religion, beyond language, beyond time.

YOUR FOOTPRINTS ON MY HEART
(PART 2)

You've touched my spirit in a way no earthly being can
You've given me a bright new dawn, a fresh start
You've empowered me, now I'm stronger when I stand
I thank You for bringing Your light to my heart.

You've given me warm sunshine
and rainbows after the rain
You've given me hope when all around me fell apart
You've allowed me to blossom and grow,
to heal after the hurt and pain
I thank You for leaving Your footprints on my heart.

You are the Beacon of Light I can turn to when in despair
For you are the Glorious Whole, and I am a mere part
You are the Loving Hand to dry my tears with such care
I thank You for leaving Your footprints on my heart.

THE MAESTRO

Words cannot describe the emotions felt within
As I watch and hear the renowned maestro perform live.
My eyes fill with tears when I hear
his guitar, when I see him,
I am awakened, I am in awe - I feel alive.

Words cannot describe the stirrings of my heart
As I hear Vicente Amigo deftly, passionately perform.
I hear the rhythmic cajon, the zealous canto,
the flamenco art -
A dream has been realized -
I feel, I breathe the duende - I am reborn.

Words cannot describe the joy in my soul,
As I hear Vicente's guitar, his every precious song.
I hear his passion, his perfect grace,
each piece he plays makes me whole -
Here with the sounds of flamenco, this is where I belong.

THE BACKWATERS OF POOVAR

I reflect on the quiet backwaters of Poovar,
A place of unblemished beauty.
I allow my mind to sway with every coconut palm,
To move softly with the wind, to be free.

I yearn for Poovar, for all its stillness and peace,
I yearn for the gentle flowing water, the unpolluted sky,
For the majesty of the forest, the enduring trees,
For the doe-eyed wildlife, the lone bird's cry.
My heart is held captive -
But Poovar holds the key for its release.

I yearn for Poovar, for its untold beauty and peace,
I long to observe the simple life of the people,
To look them kindly in the eye,
To immerse myself in the sweet language they speak.
I yearn for the gentle flowing water, for the clear blue sky,
I yearn to visit again and to never say goodbye.

FADO

Fado, with nostalgia woven into each tune
Brings a tear to the eye, across the cheek.
Fado, the song of the Sun wooing the Moon
Asking for its love to be requited soon.

Fado, the song of the yearning heart
The song moving across mountains and oceans
The song of pain, of longing that strikes the heart
Of the heartbroken lovers miles apart.

Fado, the song of the restless soul
Meanders its way through my heart
And the honeyed voice mends my soul
Piece by piece, until it's whole.

Fado, the song of the Sun wooing the Moon
Asking for its love to be requited soon.

AN ODE TO GRANADA

Granada, oh how you mesmerize,
With rolling hills and snow-capped mountains.
Your beauty lasts forever in the mind's eye,
With blooming gardens and shimmering fountains.

Granada, oh you capture my restless heart,
With history, culture and intricate design.
I am in awe of your Moorish buildings and art,
Resilient to change and the ebb of time.

Granada, you resemble no other place -
For beliefs and cultures converge in your space
And all who visit you, stand in your shadow.

ESSAYS

"Some people make the sky more
beautiful to gaze upon.
They stay in our lives for a while,
leave footprints on our hearts,
and we are never, ever the same"

— FLAVIA WEEDN

Memories of grandfather George and the footprints he left on my soul

*"Grandfather, Great Spirit, once more behold
me on Earth and lean to hear my feeble voice"*

BLACK ELK

We go through life meeting many people, all of whom leave behind an impression, a feeling, a memory. These people pass through our lives and touch us in many ways that, unfortunately, only become clear once they have gone. If we only appreciated them more and acknowledged their love, care and consideration, life would have been a far more pleasant journey, one full of wisdom, joy and belonging. It's a sad reality that only when we lose something do we begin to fully appreciate and value it.

Alas, I never really knew the value of my grandfather George until he passed away. I was too young to understand the importance of savouring every single moment I had with him and to take full advantage of the limited time we shared. And limited time it was indeed. I was only 13, old enough to feel heartache and sorrow, young enough to openly cry. My tears fell across my cheeks unreservedly. I could not contain the emotion I felt as the imminent loss of my grandfather dawned on me. And as I watched him slowly die, I succumbed to the feelings rising within. How could something so unjust happen, something that I could not control? How could someone so dear to me be snatched away forever?

Death can be incomprehensible to someone so young. I saw it only as an injustice. A heart-breaking, painful injustice. To watch someone you love die, knowing that there is nothing you can do to keep them alive is an agony I wish for nobody. They say time will heal and for sure, 15 years later, I have healed, but there remains a faint ember of the intense pain hidden somewhere in my heart.

Perhaps this seemingly faint ember burns fiercely when I flip through the pages of the book my grandfather gave to me. A wedding gift he received decades before. Or perhaps this ember burns when I search for a word in the Oxford English Dictionary he passed on to me. Perhaps it is when I page through the Tamil-English code of conduct, the , that this faint ember burns the most. I stare at the vernacular characters and ardently yearn for the impossible: that he could have taught me our mother tongue and given me the power of such a skill.

Whatever it may be, I know that there are keepsakes in my possession that will always remind me of my grandfather and all that he meant to me. But most of all, there are many memories of him engraved in my heart that give me hope and reassurance in times of darkness and despair. It is these beautiful memories of my time with my grandfather that are engraved on my soul, like footprints in the sand.

I remember sitting at his dining room table in his home in the seaside town of Port Shepstone. There was a Parker pen and a crossword puzzle from the newspaper. I hadn't the faintest idea of how to complete a crossword puzzle or what was even involved. But it made me curious. And I enjoyed watching him trying with quiet enthusiasm to complete the puzzle. For some reason I distinctly remember my grandfather trying to teach me how to use the dictionary, an invaluable skill to any developing child. But the most distinct memory was me trying to spell the word "Portugal" and having him correct me along the way.

There were lazy summer days when I paged through reference books on his dining table and found myself engrossed. I was so completely enchanted by the images of archaeological treasures across the world and the indecipherable "grown-up" words that my grandfather eventually gave me the book to keep. It was a loving gesture I will never forget, and at times I find myself staring at the spine of on my bookshelf, yearning once more for the impossible: to have my grandfather back in my life.

Of course, as I reached the age of six and made my way to my first year at school, there were those special moments when my grandfather would walk me home and perhaps buy me the long-awaited ice-cream to savour in the simple way that only a child can. It was perhaps those quiet moments between grandfather and grandchild as they walked side by side that I remember with such affection.

A memory deeply engraved in my soul is the joyous moment when my grandfather helped me to read my first few words. It was homework time and I was burdened with the task of retracing letters in my workbook and then reading them out aloud. Simple, short words that had at first seemed so daunting, so overwhelming, became an easy task as the words flowed gently from my lips - all because of the guidance and encouragement of grandfather George.

Perhaps it was my grandfather who planted the seed of my love for reading. He was always surrounded by books, newspapers and dictionaries. And I believe he tried to foster his love of reading in me. Whenever I asked for a book of his, he never said 'no'. He passed it onto me without hesitation. Visits to the local library became a norm. The long, seemingly arduous trek to the library with my grandfather by my side was always worth the effort - I would return home clinging to newly acquired treasures and lose myself in the stories of Enid Blyton.

I believe that I too gave my grandfather moments of joy and pride. The last day of the school term always had me in a flurry of butterflies. The outcome of all my hard work and commitment would be crystallized in my end-of-term academic report. There were times when it was my grandfather who would be the first to open my report. I'd hover nearby, eagerly awaiting his response and after much scrutiny he'd fold it away with a proud smile on his face and a warm embrace for me.

The memories that bring a broad smile to my face are the evenings when my grandfather, my brother and I played cards. He always tried to cheat - not to beat us, but to simply annoy us. And he succeeded because we always protested and fought with him in a loving manner that only grandchildren and grandparents would know and relate to. Playing cards was by no means a frivolous activity. He diligently kept score all through the night. Eventually we would retire to bed, defeated once more by our grandfather, but content nonetheless.

There was one hot, humid December afternoon that we spent with family and friends on a North Coast farm. We picked fresh litchis off the tree and relished the beauty of nature all around us. I will never forget the sight of my grandfather being so happy with us, his family. And now as I stare at a photograph of him standing next to me for my fourth birthday, I earnestly wish to be transported back to that beautiful time to hold his warm, protective hand once more and tell him how much I love and adore him.

I will never know the joy of seeing the expression on his face as I hand him the anthologies of poetry I have au-thored and published, for him to know that all his efforts to instil the love of reading and writing in me were not in vain. I will never be able to see the joy in his eyes as he beholds the responsible, trustworthy and principled people that my brother and I have grown into.

But what I do know for sure is that my grandfather watches from above and he sees all that I have become, all that my brother has become and perhaps he looks down upon us with pride and love. What I do know for sure is that the most beautiful memories I have of my grandfather are locked away in my heart, engraved on my soul like footprints that last forever.

Esther's prayer

*"Too often we underestimate the power of a
touch, a smile, a kind word, a listening ear,
an honest compliment, or the smallest act
of caring, all of which have the potential
to turn a life around"*

Leo Buscaglia

She walks into the room with ease and there is a notice-able mark of unembellished elegance and grace in her gait. There's a sweet smile on her face as she saunters towards me and suddenly I realize that I'm in capable hands. She has done this task countless times before, yet I can sense that she takes the time and makes the effort to get to know every woman who sits before her.

She greets me warmly and ensures I am seated comfortably at the table. She brings a bowl of water at a lukewarm temperature and gently starts cleansing my hands. Her hands are warm, her skin is soft and supple - a telltale sign of her daily occupation. Within minutes, a connection sparks between us and I'm drawn into the magnetic glow and warmth of Esther's smile as she begins the pampered manicure.

Esther is a lady with physical traits that one would least expect to see in the southern states of India. She is Nepalese. The moment she reveals this part of her identity to me, everything about her appearance makes sense. She has wide set, almond-shaped eyes that have a soft, radiant light that comes from within. Her skin is smooth, slightly freckled and almost flawless with a light maple sugar hue. Her dark brown hair is neatly tied away from her face, but I can see that as it falls from her ponytail it is wavy with a slight frizz.

She is a Christian and proud to be so. Her faith is evident in practically every turn of our conversation. She oozes with an affection for the Divine and an admiration for God's all-encompassing power. She so readily tells me how her grandparents converted to Christianity when a missionary came to their village in Nepal many years ago, and how she has always been content to follow the Christian way of life.

I am mesmerized by her ability to engage with such ease with a perfect stranger. I admire how she connects so effortlessly, with someone so different, someone from a different continent, from a totally different culture and religion. I sense that she can somehow see right through me and that she understands me without really knowing who I am.

Esther says that she can tell from my face that I am a good girl and I deserve to have a good husband one day, someone who will look after me well and treat me with kindness and respect. I giggle at her straightforwardness, and perhaps I blush slightly at her generous, unassuming words, knowing that I am certainly a long way from finding that person. Indeed, Esther surprises me with her whole-hearted warmth when she states, "I will pray for you. I will pray for you to find a good husband who will look after you and make you happy."

Her candid tenderness with me, a stranger, ignites a flame of fondness within my heart towards this over-whelmingly optimistic woman. She enquires about my education, my job, my family, my sibling. She wants to know more when I tell her about my brother's recent wedding. Her questions are seemingly endless. "What did you wear? Did you wear a saree? What did the bride wear? Is she beautiful? How is your relationship with your brother's wife?"

She is elated when I reveal to her that they are happily married, and my sister-in-law is very beautiful both on the inside and out, and we are so very close that she is more like a sister to me.

Esther is more than happy to share her own story with me when I ask. Her son is seven years old, fluent in English, Hindi and Tamil. He is progressing well in school. A clever boy. But his father could not earn a good living in India, so he went back to Nepal to work. Her son misses his father, but it is the better financial option for the family.

Esther is happily employed in Chennai. She says she would never be able to find this type of work in Nepal and would certainly not be paid as well as she is currently being paid at this renowned Indian hotel. Hence, she will continue to live here in Chennai and her son shall contin-ue to be schooled here too because the education system is better in India than in Nepal. She so proudly tells me how she has worked in this beauty parlour for nine years and that she has had the opportunity to style the hair of Hillary Clinton. It's a feather in her cap, one which she discloses with obvious pride and joy.

As she adeptly applies the second coat of the dusty rose hued nail polish to my pristinely manicured nails, she enquires about my travels in India and the next stage of the journey. She cheerfully tells me how kind, tolerant and good natured the Tamil-speaking people of South India are, how beautiful the Tamil language is. She says the South Indian people are very peaceful and loving, and as she shares this sentiment with me, I feel a surge of endearment towards this woman sitting before me, knowing that I have my roots in this part of India, that my ancestors were these peaceful and kind Tamil-speaking people, whom she so affectionately speaks of.

Esther gradually comes to the end of my manicure and as we wait for the final coat of clear nail polish to dry, she reassures me one last time. She tells me that I should not have any worries, that she will pray for me to find a good, decent boy to marry and she will pray for me to have a happy life.

I am touched by her simple, unpretentious yet thoughtful words. Although I am a stranger to her, she has taken the time to get to know me within the past hour. She has taken the time to connect with me, to look me in the eye and see me for the person I really am - an act which many people who are so seemingly close to me have not yet done. Her kind words have struck a chord deep within me. There were boundaries of faith, language, identity, age, social class and nationality between us, yet she crossed those boundaries seamlessly and her spirit gently meandered its way into my heart within a short space of 60 minutes.

Esther's beautiful smile, her genuine words and her innate kindness are a necessary reminder that there are, and will always be, good people in this world. Her smile is perhaps a sign that no matter what our geographical, physical, cultural or spiritual differences may be, we can engage with one another, we can be kind to one another and we all have the propensity to find a deep connection with a fellow human being - we all have the propensity to have a positive impact on someone else's life even if only in a little way.

And I know for sure that whenever I feel weary or low in spirit, I shall think of the warmth exuded in Esther's smile, her unbound affection, her earnest prayer. In moments of darkness and despair, the image of her radiant smile in my mind's eye will undoubtedly kindle a bright fire in my heart.

Indeed, I am ever so grateful to Esther for sharing her kind, gentle smile and conveying her heartfelt prayer for me on that late afternoon in Chennai - she truly has left a lasting imprint on my heart. In some way, it feels as though Esther did not simply pray for me alone, but for all humanity to find boundless love and joy.

Saturdays at my grandmother's table

*"If nothing is going well,
call your grandmother"*

ITALIAN PROVERB

When I reflect on all the people who have positively impacted on my sense of being, I think of one person with a rather overwhelming, somewhat indefinable feeling of affection and love. The person I think of is my maternal grandmother, my grandma Amy.

She has been the epitome of unconditional love, of unrestrained care and compassion, of the maternal thread that unwaveringly binds her family together. And the moments spent with grandma Amy are a reminder of what it is that we should strive for in life - strong familial bonds, love, commitment to our close ones, resilience, faith, humility and compassion.

There are special times on which I reflect that have given me the opportunity to bond with my maternal grandparents, to allow me to fully absorb all the love and affection that they shower upon their grandchildren.

Saturdays around my grandmother's table are those meaningful moments of resplendent sunshine when all one's worldly cares and troubles can slip away into the shadows, when life can be truly embraced for all its simple blessings.

For many years, ever since I can remember, my family have gathered in the home of my maternal grandparents on a Saturday afternoon and bonded over an unpretentious meal that was prepared with the most loving hands and heart. It is perhaps those moments that we share at my grandmother's table, over a comforting plate of her traditional South Indian chicken curry that have allowed me to feel a deep sense of belonging and love.

Indeed, it is this deep sense of belonging which is so difficult to find in our modern era of broken homes, dysfunctional families and isolated, narcissistic lives. The moments we share around my grandmother's table are timeless and are etched across my memory. These are the moments of laughter, light and joy which make the oftentimes stressful, burdensome and mundane episodes of everyday life tolerable and easier to surmount. I shall share these precious times with you so that you may in some way know and understand the enduring beauty of sitting at my grandmother's table.

It is the simple deed of entertaining my six-year-old cousin, playing an intricate board game with him or assembling a children's puzzle he has done countless times before. Or to cheerfully read a book with him about a dinosaur. Or the patient way in which I teach him how to spell a word beyond his age, which he grasps so effortlessly and can skilfully recite to me a few minutes later (the word is 'butterfly'). I take the time to teach him how to look at a clock and tell the time, to draw the hands on a blank clock. "It is six o'clock, so where will the small hand go?" They may seem like arduous tasks to one who cannot have patience with a child, but for me it is a priceless, treasured opportunity to bond with the little boy I am privileged to call my cousin.

It is the relaxed conversation I have with my grandfather as he enquires about work. He knows precisely how far to go with his questions - asking just enough to show he cares, just enough to not prod and pry. Curious about my writing, he asks about the newsletter that I edit and compile for the company and the next anthology of poetry I will author.

And of course, once the plates are cleared and the dishes have been washed, it is my task to make everybody a good cup of tea. By now I know exactly how milky my grandmother has her tea, how many teaspoons of sugar my aunt takes, how full the cup should be for my little cousin, the specific colour of my grandfather's cup. Their preferences have become a sort of familial knowledge engraved in my head.

And all the while as the tea is brewed, I am regaled with stories, from the past and present. Stories of my grandparents' early years of marriage, the burdens of being married and becoming parents at a young age, as well as the moments of happiness as a growing family. We laugh together at the colourful, humorous tales, and stare in astonishment at the moving tales of hardship and pain. My grandmother delights us with stories of living in a far-away farm in Tugela, surrounded by fruit trees and cane fields, living by candle light and without the amenities we have grown so accustomed to in modern life.

She tells us of how difficult it was to be married when mutual respect was not always given, and that thoughts, opinions and emotions were not always considered. She describes to us how a midwife delivered her babies late at night, with no access to the paediatric care and hygiene of a hospital. She recounts how on many occasions a bout of marital conflict prompted her to pack a suitcase and travel the long distance to her mother's home in Pietermaritzburg with two young children by her side. I have nothing but admiration for her resilience and her immense strength of character to have overcome so many of life's struggles.

I smile as my grandmother suggests (well, more like commands) that I should not marry young, that I should enjoy life as a single and free individual, that marriage has its fair share of misery just as much as it may bring happiness. Certainly, it is a hard-to-swallow fact that my grandmother as well as her two daughters (my aunt and my mother) did not have the opportunity of receiving a full education. Taken out of school as young teenagers, the opportunity to upskill and develop themselves was never given - the choice was regrettably not theirs to make. Perhaps it is a reminder of the patriarchal society that once dictated the path of a woman's life, of the inequitable social norms that once prevailed, of the inescapable social pressure for women to be confined to the kitchen and to have an ever-swelling womb.

It is perhaps a necessary reminder that I should have nothing but gratitude for the opportunities generously bestowed on me - the opportunity to be educated, to have my voice heard, to make choices of my own, to give life to my talents, interests and skills, all of which the women of my family in generations before did not have.

Nonetheless, all the worldly opportunities and ideals I possess are forgotten when I sit at my grandmother's table. I am governed only by humility, a sense of belonging and unrestrained joy. The simple act of being present in a home of genuine love and boundless affection is all that matters - not a university degree, a favourable bank balance or a sophisticated job.

And as I gaze upon my grandmother, with her glowing smile and her shining eyes I know that she is a blessing I have perhaps taken for granted. I am afraid of the day that is sure to come when we must say goodbye. I know I will sorely miss those treasured days when she lovingly prepares my favourite Indian sweetmeat, the gulab jamun, in an almost perfect manner - indeed it is nothing but a magical amalgamation of sugar, condensed milk, cardamom and coconut.

I ponder about who will then teach me those wise lessons she has conveyed to me over the years - that it is good to be kind, caring and loving to others no matter how different they are from you, no matter what history of hurt and pain lies between you, no matter how callous or insensitive they have been. And even though I am yet to action her pearls of wisdom in my life, I know that one day I will value and give life to the powerful advice she has imparted. I reflect on how I will experience moments at my grandmother's table, without my grandmother. What will life be without her?

I know that once she goes, there will be no one as beautiful and loving as her to fill the dark void of her absence. Hence, I make a sincere promise to myself today that I shall from now on cherish every moment I have with my grandparents and be truly mindful of all the light one experiences when seated around my grandmother's table on a Saturday afternoon. For it is the love and sweet joy I feel when I am seated at my grandmother's table that have left some of the deepest impressions on my heart.

———————————

The End

www.ingramcontent.com/pod-product-compliance
Lightning Source LLC
Chambersburg PA
CBHW031353060726
47590CB00007B/2769